BAD KITTY
Drawn to
TROUBLE

NICK BRUEL

A NEAL PORTER BOOK

ROARING BROOK PRESS

New York

For this, the tenth Bad Kitty book, I would like to acknowledge the invaluable support I have always received from the good folk at Roaring Brook who have supported me and my ornery pussycat from the very beginning. Special attention must be given to Simon Boughton, Lauren Wohl, the ever-patient Jennifer Browne, who has designed each of these books, and, of course, my often invoked editor, Neal Porter. Likewise, nothing would have been possible over the years without their assistants Ben Tomek, Kat Kopit, Colleen AF Venable, and Emily Feinberg to name just a few. Within the walls of Macmillan, Roaring Brook's parent company, there are simply too many names for me to acknowledge, and to be perfectly honest I don't know them all even though I should. But to the many people in marketing, publicity, sales, design, and so forth . . . thank you. Your participation in Bad Kitty's growth and success has been critical. So, from the bottom of my heart, thank you.

Copyright © 2014 by Nick Bruel
A Neal Porter Book
Published by Roaring Brook Press
Roaring Brook Press is a division of Holtzbrinck Publishing Holdings Limited Partnership
175 Fifth Avenue, New York, New York 10010
mackids.com

Library of Congress Cataloging-in-Publication Data

Bruel, Nick, author, illustrator
Bad Kitty drawn to trouble / Nick Bruel. — First edition.
    p. cm
  "A Neal Porter Book."
  Summary: Author/illustrator Nick Bruel tries to explain to the reader how to write a story, but Bad Kitty is not at all happy about the plot, which has her going on a turnip diet to lose weight. Includes a recipe for roasted turnips.
  ISBN 978-1-59643-671-8
  [1. Cats—Fiction. 2. Authorship—Fiction. 3. Illustration of books—Fiction. 4. Humorous stories.]
  I. Title.
  PZ7.B82832Bal 2013
  [E]—dc23
                                                          2013001633

Roaring Brook Press books may be purchased for business or promotional use. For information on bulk purchases please contact Macmillan Corporate and Premium Sales Department at (800) 221-7945 x5442 or by email at specialmarkets@macmillan.com.

First edition 2014
Printed in the United States of America by RR Donnelley
& Sons Company, Harrisonburg, Virginia
1   3   5   7   9   10   8   6   4   2

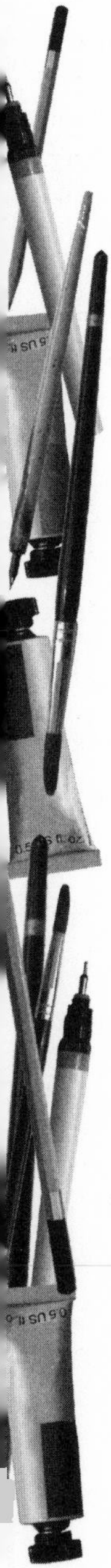

• CONTENTS •

CHAPTER ONE

MEET THE AUTHOR

Hi.

My name is Nick Bruel.

I am an AUTHOR,★ which means that I write books.

In fact, I wrote THIS book.

This one. The book you're reading right now.

Now, smell the book you're holding. That's right. Smell it.

Does it smell like paper? That's how you know it's a book.

If you are reading this book on an electronic device, please download an app that will make your book smell like paper. Then you'll know what I'm talking about.

All words followed by a ★ will be defined in the Appendix at the end of this book.

Don't you think it would be nicer if you could see me? After all, I can see YOU. So, I think it would be nicer if we could see each other.

Like all children's book authors, I am extremely good-looking. But I'm not sure how you could see that for yourself.

I know! I'll make a drawing of myself!

As you can see, I am also an ILLUSTRATOR,★ which means that I made all the artwork, also known as "illustrations," in this book.

Hmmmm . . . I'm not sure if this is good enough.

What to do? What to do?

Hey, I know! I'll draw a mirror! Then I'll look into the mirror and you can see me!

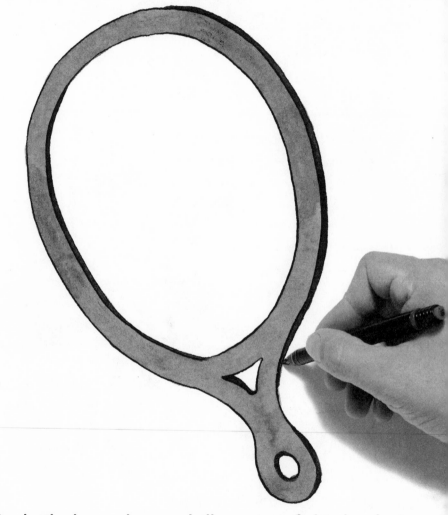

As both the author and illustrator of this book, I can do anything I want.

HI THERE!

Now
I can
see you,
and you can
see me!

I told you I was good-
looking. Now stop staring at
me! Didn't your mother ever tell
you that staring at good-looking
people for too long can make
you go color blind? No? Really?
Well, that's what my mother always told me.

She also told me that watching too many cartoons would make me wet the bed. And, boy, was she ever right about that! Although, I do think the quart of orange juice I drank every night might have had something to do with that.

ACTUAL PHOTO OF THE AUTHOR IN FIRST GRADE

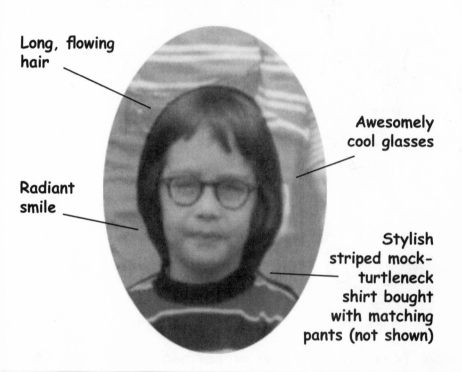

Long, flowing hair

Awesomely cool glasses

Radiant smile

Stylish striped mock-turtleneck shirt bought with matching pants (not shown)

But enough about my personal life! We have important work to do!

This is a BAD KITTY book, and we haven't even seen Kitty yet!

I'm going to start drawing Kitty now. You can draw Kitty with me if you want. I'll draw on the left, but I'll leave you enough room on the right so you can follow each step. If you are reading from a library book, you may want to ask your librarian first if you can draw on the pages.* If you are reading from a digital copy of this book, go ahead and draw on the screen; your parents won't mind.**

1. Draw her nose.

2. Draw her mouth.

3. Draw her elbows. No, wait! I meant eyes. Draw her eyes. Sorry.

4. Now draw the hair on her head.

* Your librarian is going to say going to say "No."
** Yes, they will.

Are you exhausted yet? No? Really. Well, I am. I need some water. I'm going to go get a glass of water and come right back.

Ahhh . . . that's better. You're still here? But I was gone an hour! Don't you have homework or something? Fine. Where were we? Oh, right . . .

5. Now draw her ears.

6. And finally her whiskers.

HI, KITTY!

Shall we draw the rest of Kitty? Yes? Well, too bad. Because I don't feel like it. HAH! Just kidding! I'm funny. Wasn't I funny just now? I thought I was very funny. Everyone loves me because I'm funny. Didn't you think I was . . . um . . . okay. Moving on.

7. Next we draw Kitty's elbows. I mean NECK! Neck. Sorry.

8. Draw her shoulders and front paws.

Don't forget about that little tuft of white fur on her chest.

9. Now her back legs and paws.

10. And finally her tail.

That wasn't so hard, was it? Now draw her about a billion more times and you'll know what my job is like.

13

You'll probably want to practice drawing Kitty so here's what you can do . . . Just photocopy pages 10 through 13 and keep drawing her over and over just as I showed you. But don't tell my editor. He won't like this idea one bit.

Too late! He found out!

Which one of you told him?

Let's see now. Something is still not quite right.

It's as if something is still missing. But what can it be? We drew her eyes. We drew that little tuft of white fur on her chest. Maybe she needs more elbows. No, that's not it.

Kitty, can you think of what's missing?

Oh, right! We still have to give you color! Silly me. Just wait here a minute, Kitty, while I go get my paints.

Okey dokey, Kitty. Hold still while I apply some colors to you.

As you can see, I use a veritable rainbow of colors to paint Kitty.

Her fur is jet black. Her nose is cadmium red, shaded with red earth. Her eyes are cadmium yellow, shaded with yellow ochre. Her mouth is flesh toned and shaded with brown pink. And the white tuft of fur on her chest is highlighted with a hint of cobalt blue.

What's that? You can't see all of these beautiful colors? What about the yellow ochre? The cadmium red? The cobalt blue? Can't you see ANY of them?!

EGADS!
You've gone COLOR BLIND!

I told you not to stare at my picture too long!

· CHAPTER TWO ·
MEET THE CHARACTER★

Okay. Let's get started!

We're lucky! We already have a character for our story. That's YOU, Kitty!

Yes, YOU! You are someone who has a personality, and as our story moves forward we're going to get to know you better.

In fact, Kitty, you're not just any character. You're going to be this story's PROTAGONIST,★ which is a fancy word that means you'll be the most important character in this story.

It's a bit like being the star in a movie.

I thought you might like that, Kitty.

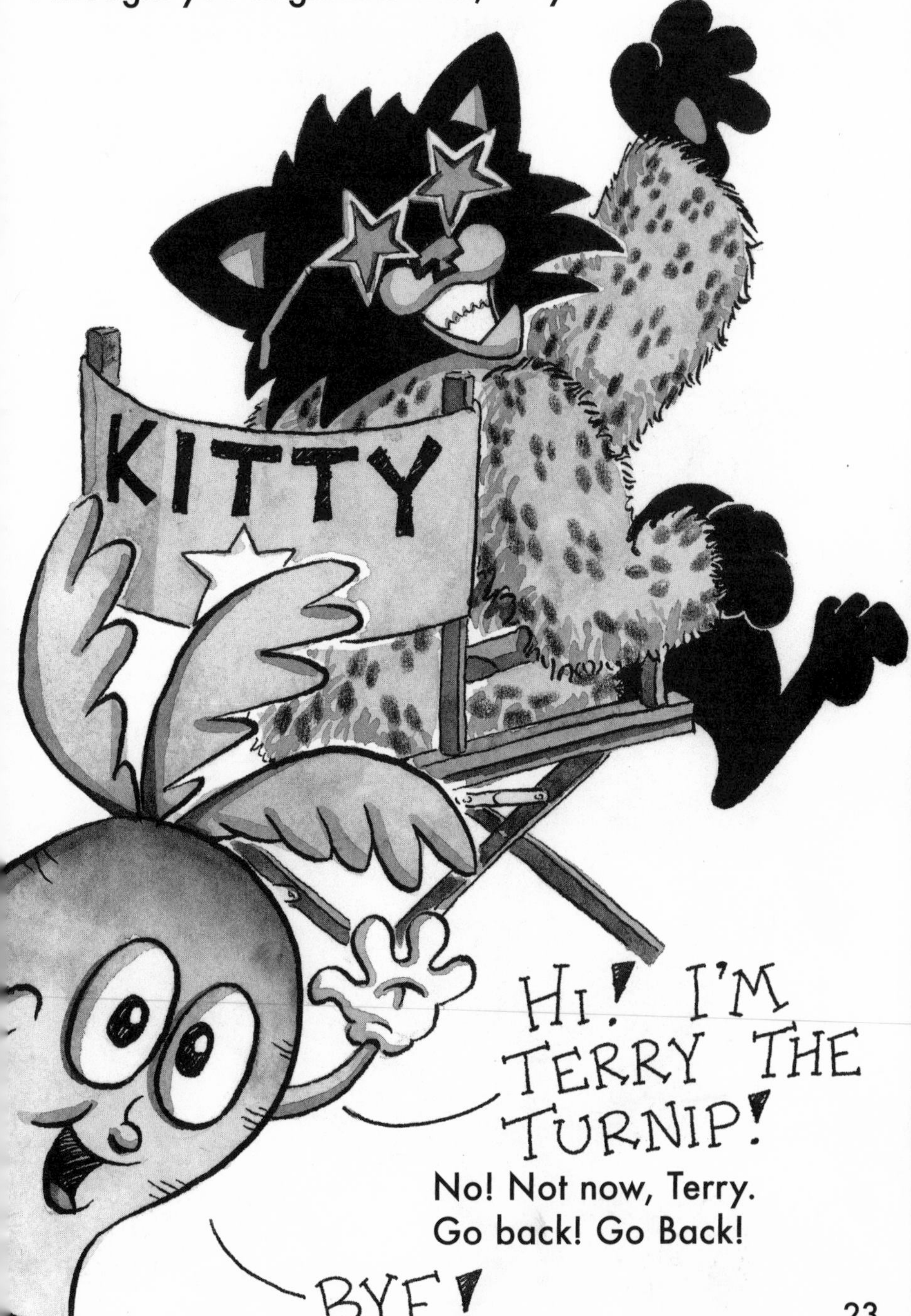
KITTY
HI! I'M TERRY THE TURNIP!
BYE!

No! Not now, Terry.
Go back! Go Back!

Terry? Don't worry about him, Kitty. That was just a little FORESHADOWING,★ which is when a writer drops little hints about what's going to come later in the story.

But right now we need a SETTING,★ someplace where your story can take place.

Deciding on a setting is one great way to start a story.

For instance, maybe our story will be a great pirate adventure! In that case, we might set our story in the middle of the ocean!

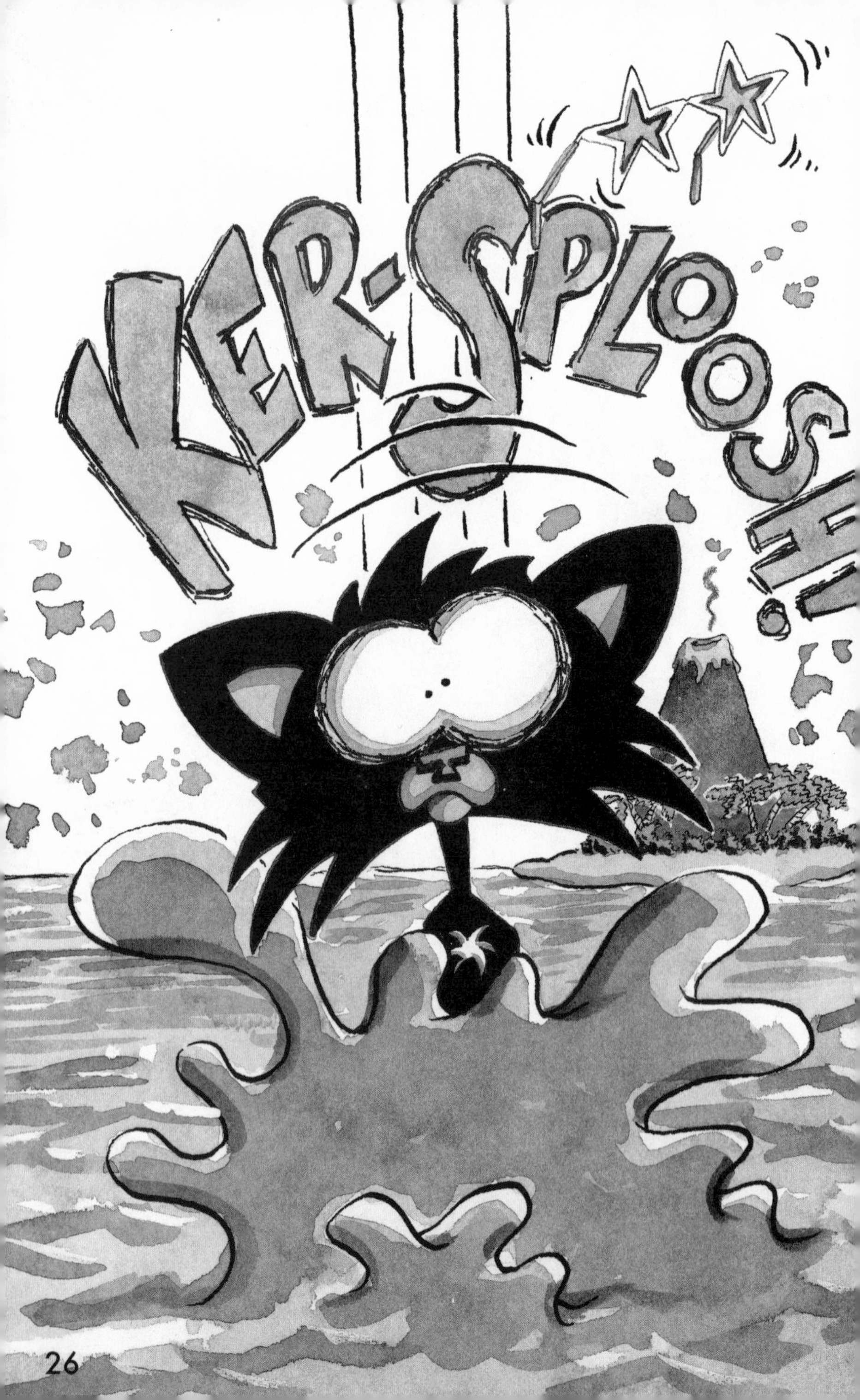
KER-SPLOOSH!

Oops. Sorry about that, Kitty. Here . . .
let me help you up.

So ocean adventure was a bad idea. But don't worry, Kitty. We'll think of something. Maybe we could set our story in the jungle.

Sure! We'll make an exotic jungle tale set inside the wild, untamed forests of Africa with strange plants, mysterious noises, and huge, dangerous beasts of prey.

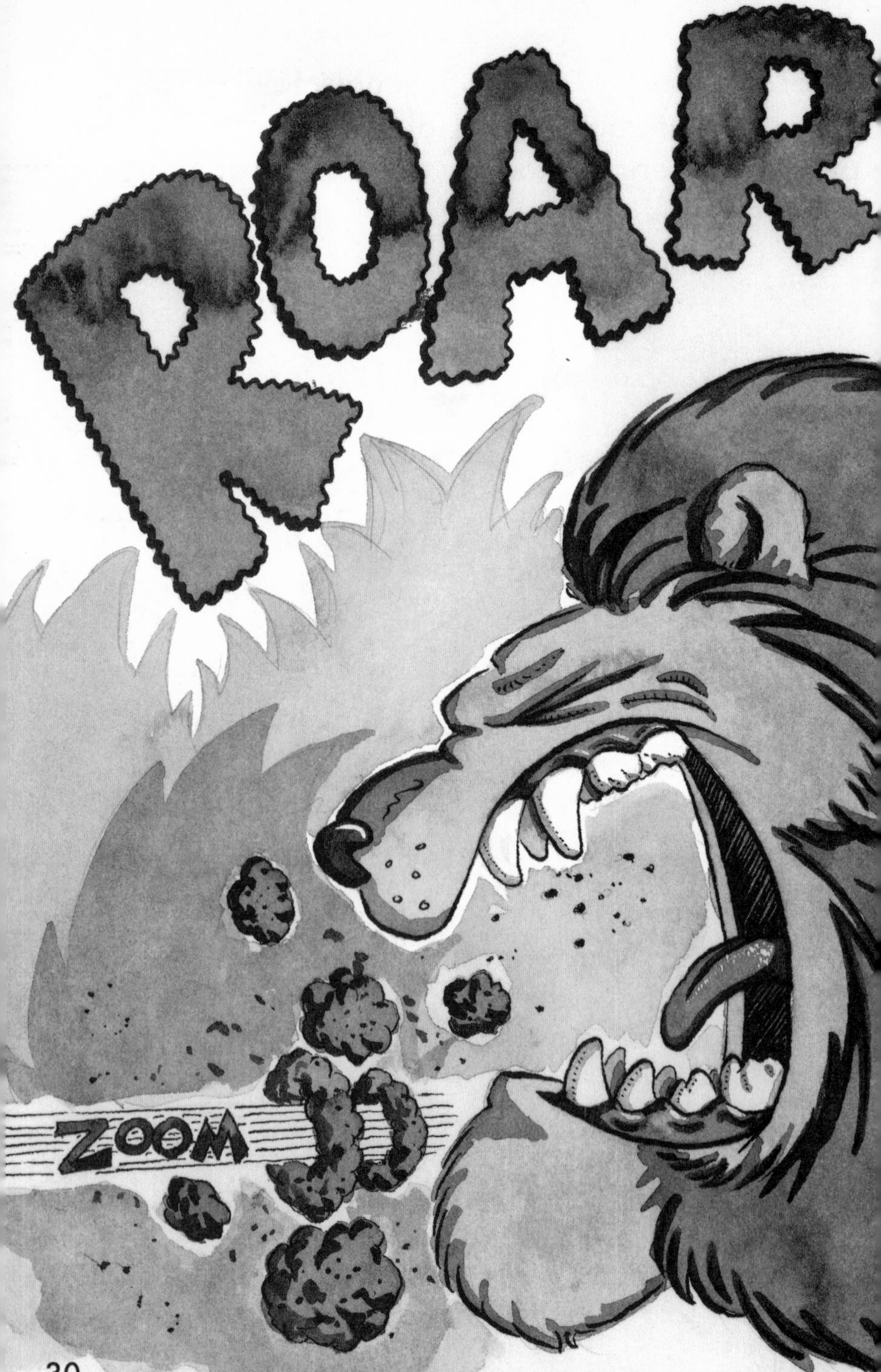
ROAR
ZOOM

What's wrong, Kitty? Don't you like this setting?

HI! I'M TERRY...

Not now, Terry!

BYE!

Fine. Maybe we could set our story in the frozen North. That would be different.

SCREECH

Or maybe a spooky graveyard! Readers never seem to get tired of a good zombie story.

You know what . . . We could use all three settings. In most stories, the settings change.

But, NAH! I think we should stick with the same old setting we usually use in your stories, Kitty: your home.

You're a cat, after all, Kitty. And cats usually live inside a house. Sometimes, it's important that the setting match the character to make the story believable.

AND TO THINK THAT I GAVE UP A "BABY MOUSE" AUDITION TO BE HERE!

MY AGENT IS NOT GOING TO BE HAPPY ABOUT THIS!

Of course, a story doesn't always have to be believable to be good.

• CHAPTER THREE •

THE CONFLICT

So now we have a protagonist and we have a setting for our story. But a story just isn't a story until something happens. But how do we make something happen?

Well, let's think about our protagonist—Kitty. If we want to write a story about her, we need to get to know her better.

Let's begin by asking ourselves some questions about Kitty . . .

> What does Kitty like?
> What does Kitty NOT like?
> What makes her happy?
> What makes her angry?
> What is she afraid of?

Asking questions like these about your protagonist is one of the most important things you can do when you're writing a story. Because when you find the answers, you just may find your story.

I know one thing that Kitty cares about. She likes food. So, let's think about that.

Hey, I know what we can do! Let's make a MACGUFFIN!* What's that, you ask? A MacGuffin is a goal or desired object that a character in a story really wants. In this case, I think Kitty would really want a big bowl of her favorite FOOD. So let's give her some.

BOI-OI-OI-OI-OING!

KITTY

But here's the problem . . . If we just give Kitty the food, and then she eats her food, then there really won't be much of a story.

What we need to do is create a little CONFLICT.*

Conflict is what happens when a character faces a problem or a challenge. Without conflict, a story would be very dull, indeed. So let's not make it so easy for Kitty to get what she wants.

Sorry, Kitty, but you're getting too fat. We've decided that you need to eat less.

But here's the good news! Our story is starting to take shape! In fact, I think we can now give it a title . . .

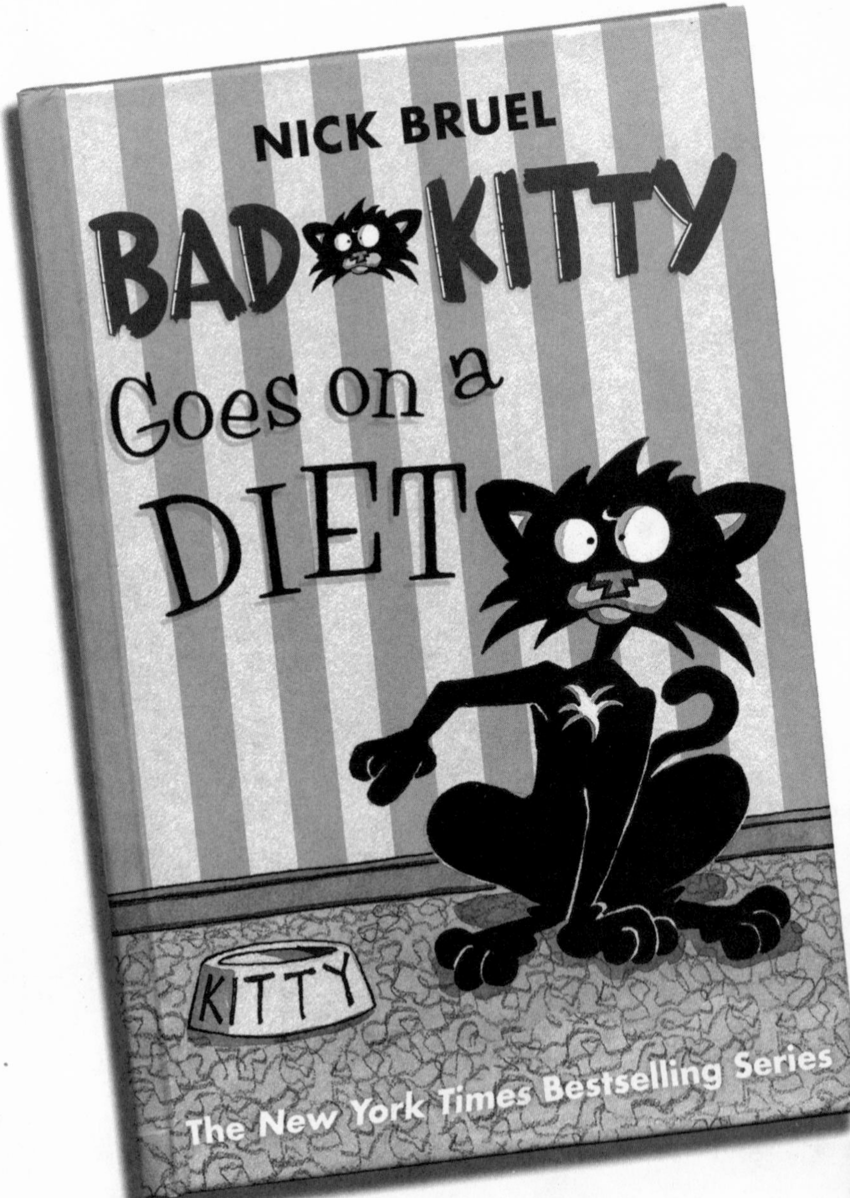
NICK BRUEL
BAD KITTY
Goes on a
DIET
KITTY
The New York Times Bestselling Series

Wow. Doesn't this look like it could become a great story, Kitty? Are you as excited as I am?

You see, Kitty, often the conflict that a character like yourself faces can become the PLOT* to the story. The plot is simply what happens in a story. And the plot to this story will be about what happens when you don't get the breakfast you want.

Gosh, Kitty. You can be such a harsh critic sometimes.

But going on a diet doesn't mean that you have to go hungry, Kitty. Here ya go!

This is great! Our story has a plot. But I think it can use a THEME.* If you going on a diet is the plot, then maybe the turnip can be the theme. Hmmm . . . that doesn't sound right. Maybe the cat food is the theme. No. The polar bear? No.

You know what, Kitty, I'm embarrassed to say this, but I don't think I know what a "theme" is. Well, who better to turn to than our very own answer man: Uncle Murray.

OH, UNCLE MURRAY!

TURNIP

UNCLE MURRAY'S FUN FACTS

WHAT'S THE DIFFERENCE BETWEEN PLOT AND THEME?

YAY! I love, love, LOVE to write stories!!

Hi, Uncle Murray. I need some help with how to write a story.

I'll do what I can, Boss.

So, to begin . . . What is a plot?

The plot is what the story is about.

Okay, then what is a theme?

The theme is what the story is about.

Wait . . . WHAT? Are you trying to tell me that the plot and the theme to a story are the same thing?

No, they're totally different. Well, kinda different. The plot describes what HAPPENS in a story. But the theme describes the ideas or the message in a story.

So what is the PLOT in our story?

Well, the plot here would be what happens when that goofy cat has to

go on a diet and doesn't get the food she wants.

And the THEME?

Well, you've been talking a lot about things like "character" and "setting" and "plot" and stuff like that. So, I think the theme here is about writing stories.

So the plot would be Kitty going on a diet and all of the goofy things that happen because of it. But the theme would be the idea of my using this story as a way of teaching kids how to write their own stories.

Now you're getting it!

So, do all stories need both a plot AND a theme?

Well, all stories need a plot. If nothing is happening, then it's not really a story. A story doesn't really need a theme to be a story. But a theme will always make a story more interesting.

Thanks, Uncle Murray. I'm going to go see how Kitty is getting along now.

Well, that certainly was interesting. Wasn't it, Kitty? Kitty?

Oh, don't be like that.

TURNIP JUICE

It's obvious you need to go on a diet, Kitty. Why just look at how much weight you've gained recently!

Trust me. You'll feel a lot better once you've lost a few pounds.

• CHAPTER FOUR •

MEET THE
ANTAGONIST

NOW?

Soon, Terry. Soon.
Just be patient.

Very few stories have only one character. They do exist, of course. But stories usually have more than one character because it's always more interesting to see how a protagonist relates to the other characters around him or her.

So I think this story will need at least one more character.

I was thinking that we could add a new character who could create a new theme for this story about the many benefits of a healthy diet. How about a friendly talking turnip named Terry who promotes good nutrition and healthy eating?

Maybe not.

But let's not forget that conflict is critical to our story. So maybe we could introduce a specific kind of character who will add to our conflict.

Let's introduce the ANTAGONIST[★] to our story!

Let's introduce the ANTAGONIST[★] to our story!

HI, PUPPY!

You're going to be our antagonist in this story!

Who's a good antagonist?! Who's a good antagonist?! You're a good antagonist! Yes, you are! Yes, you are!

Puppy, as the antagonist in this story, your role is to stand in opposition to the protagonist—that's Kitty. Often, the antagonist is the character who acts as the obstacle between the protagonist and his or her goal, or MacGuffin.

Hmmm . . . Okay, I'll make this easier.

Puppy, as the antagonist in this story your job will be to make sure Kitty stays on her diet and doesn't eat any of the food that she wants.

Let's think about this, Puppy. What would be the best way to keep Kitty away from all of this delicious looking cat food? Think hard, Puppy, because Kitty can be very crafty. Think very, very hard.

What a great idea, Puppy! You can EAT the food! I can't think of a safer place to keep Kitty's food than inside your stomach.

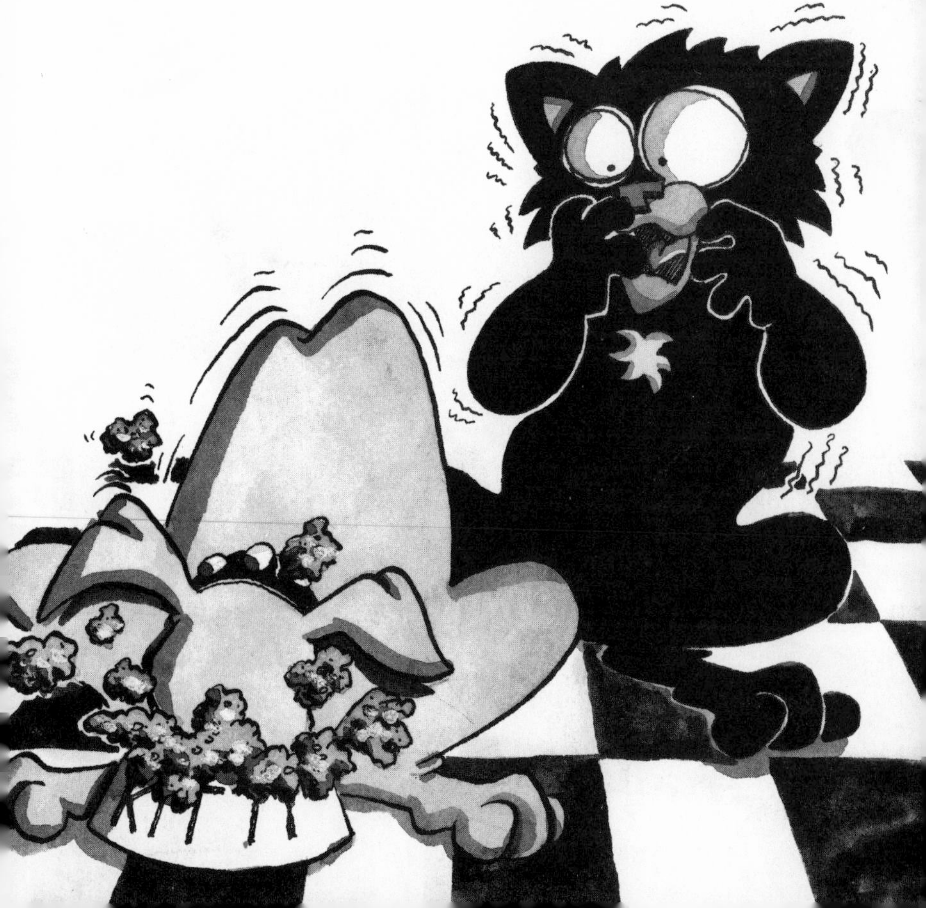

Kitty? Are you all right? You suddenly don't look so well. Do you need to lie down?

Don't worry! I'll quickly draw a pillow for you to fall onto. It's right there in front of you.

Oops.

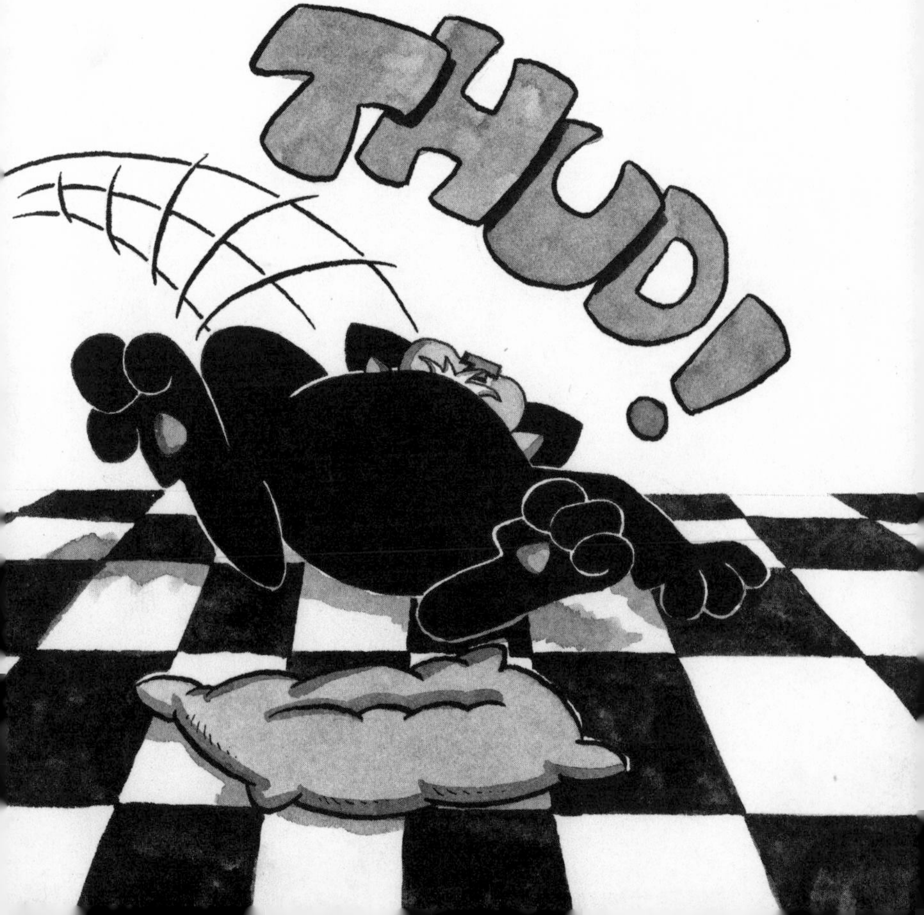
THUD!

• CHAPTER FIVE •

PLOT POINTS

KITTY! OHHHH, KITTEEEEEEEEE!

Gosh, Puppy. I can't wake her. Maybe you could try something.

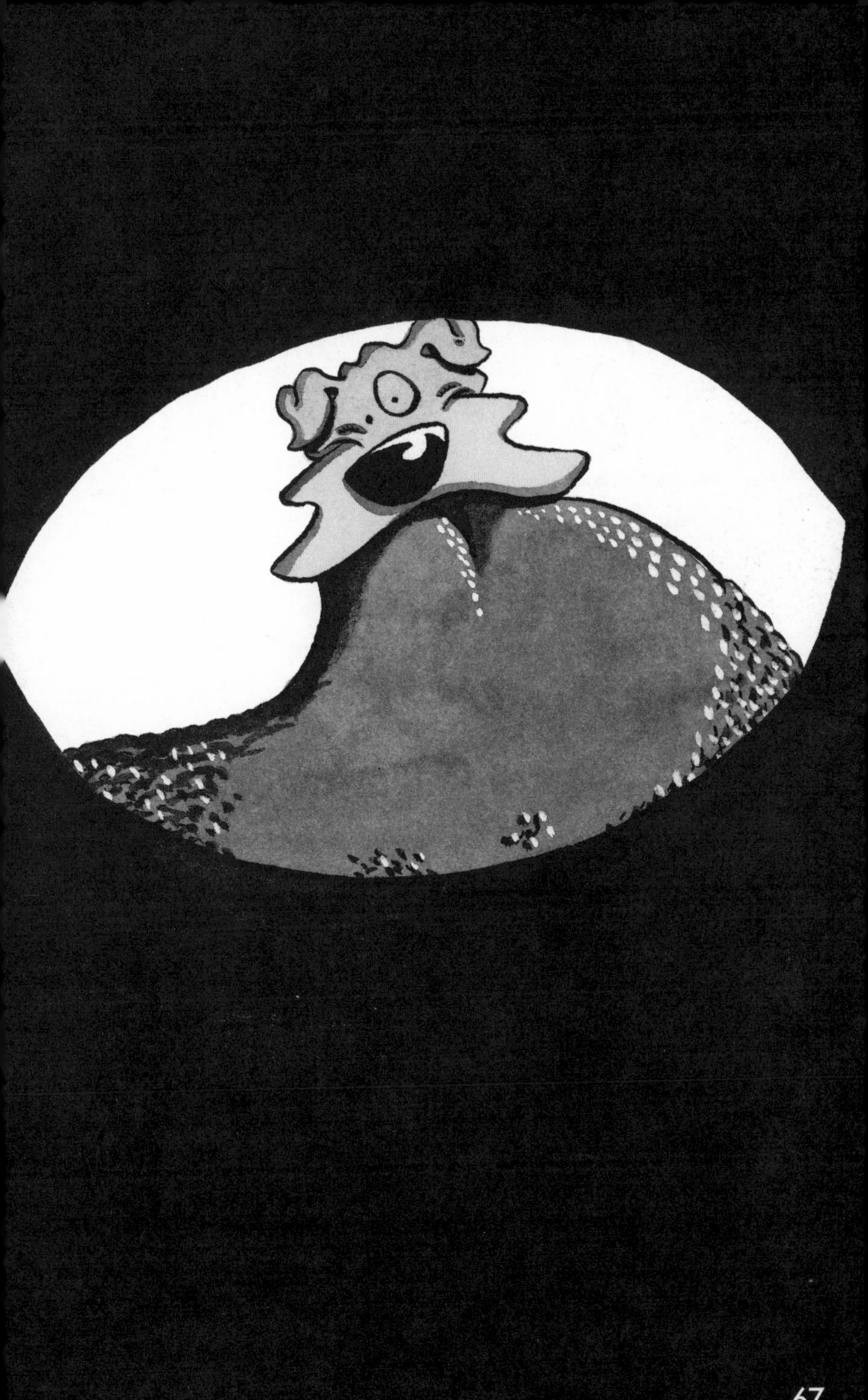

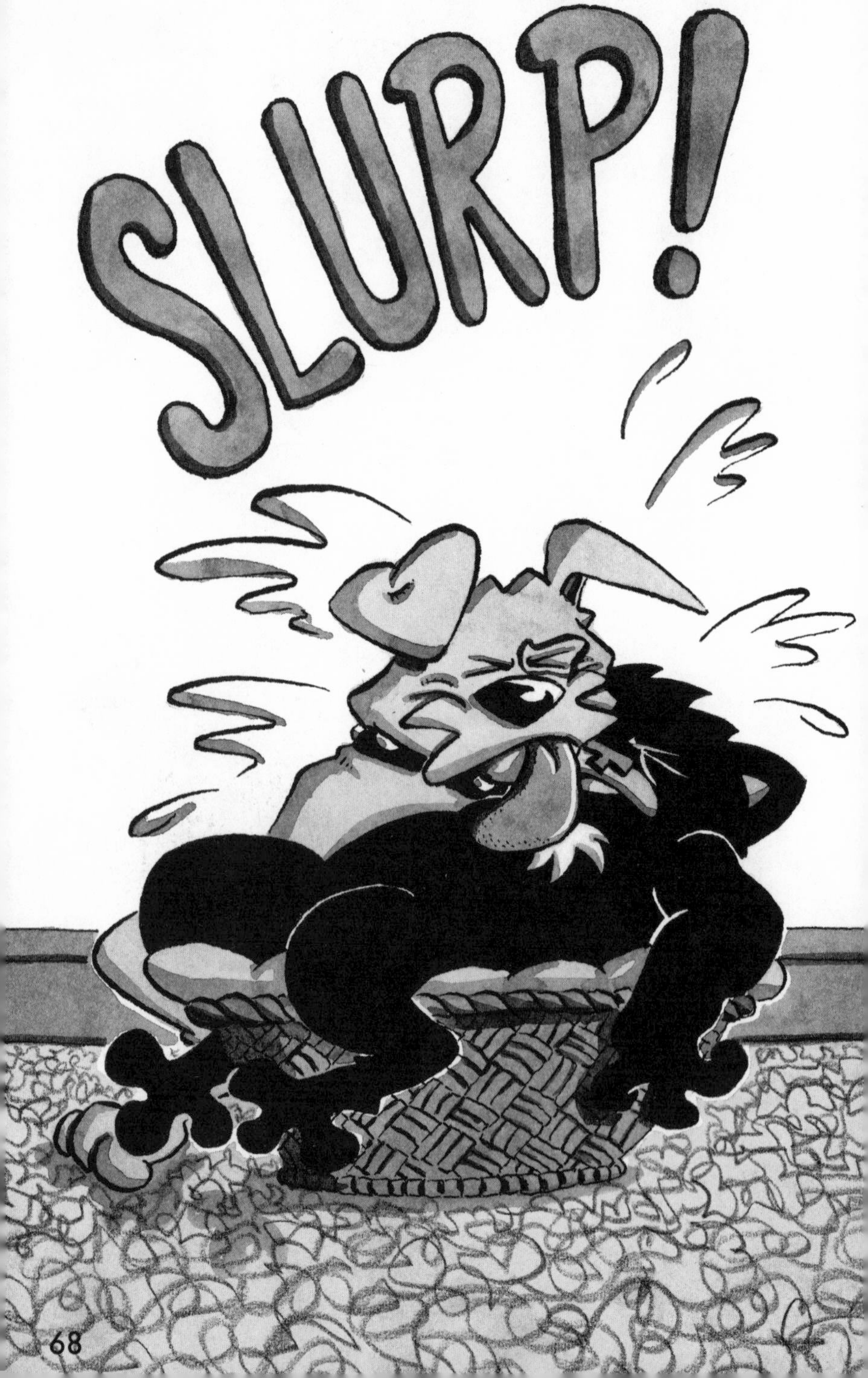
SLURP!

GOOD JOB, PUPPY!

That did the trick!

Welcome back, Kitty. You had us worried when you passed out like that. But you also did us a real big favor! You introduced the first PLOT POINT* to our story!

SPURT!

A plot point is a moment or event of some sort in which your story can take a sudden or unexpected turn. A good story should always have at least one plot point. Many stories will have lots of them. And we got one when you suddenly passed out!

Do you get it, Kitty? When you passed out, you gave us a point at which our plot changed. So while the plot of our story used to be just about keeping you on a diet, now our plot can also be about helping you to recover from your terrible shock.

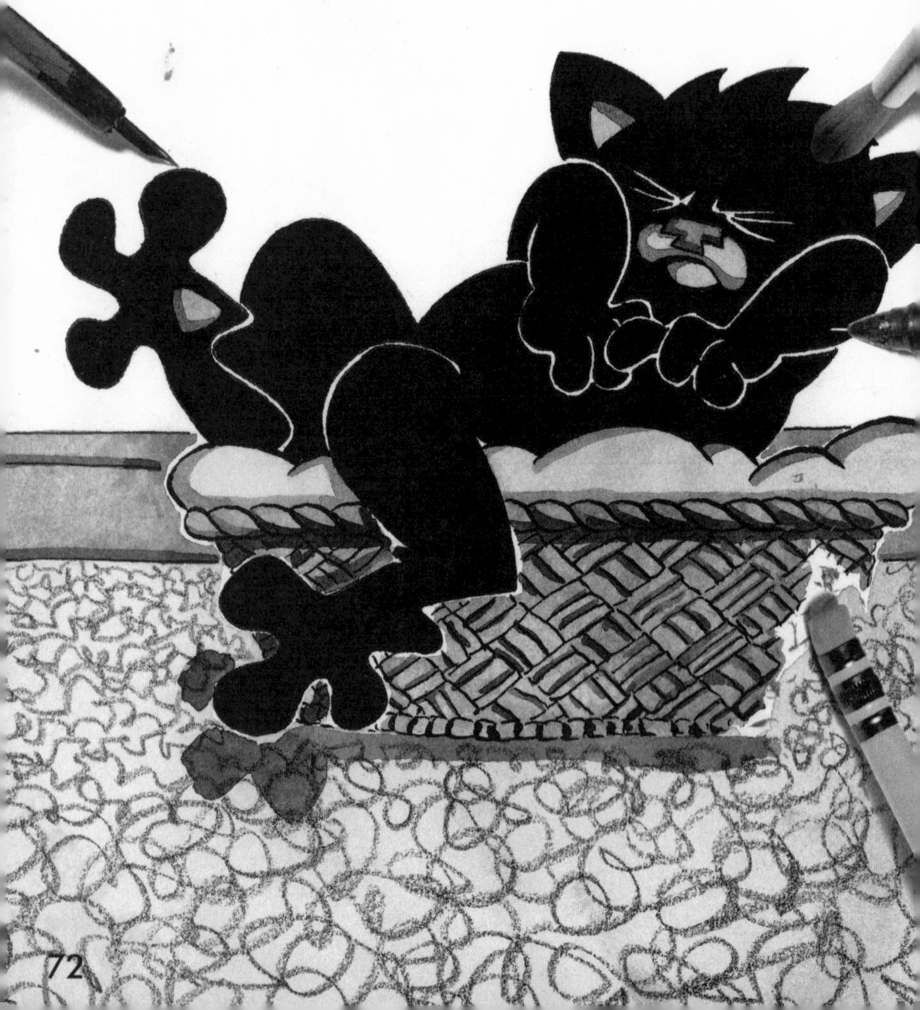

There you go, Kitty. You'll feel better in no time!

Hmmm . . . Maybe we should change the title of our story to . . .

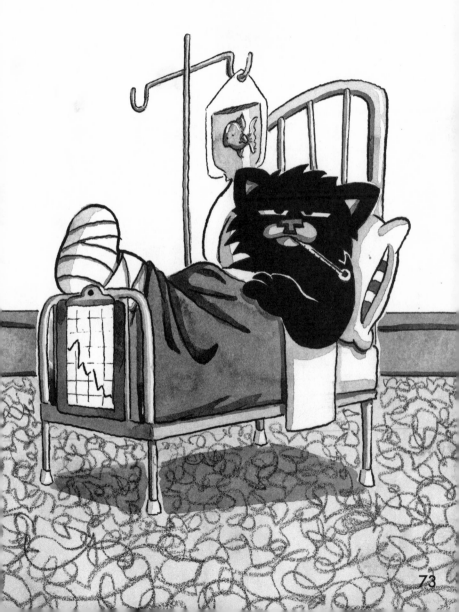

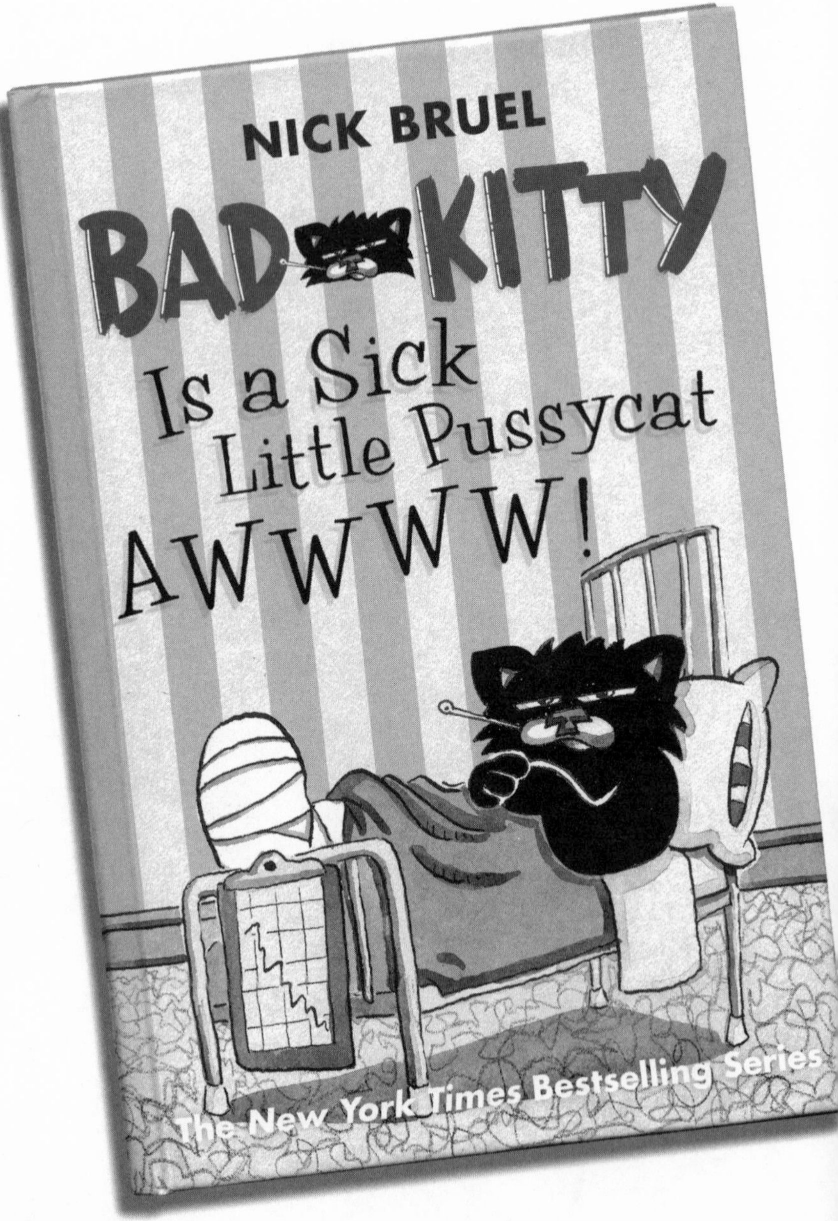
NICK BRUEL
BAD KITTY
Is a Sick Little Pussycat
AWWWW!
The New York Times Bestselling Series

And, of course, the one thing you'll need to fully recover from your illness will be a nice, hot, steaming glass of delicious turnip juice.

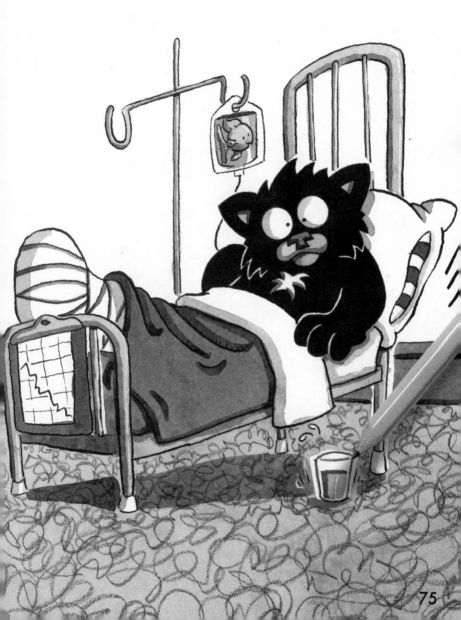

HEY! WHAT THE . . . !
LET GO OF THAT!

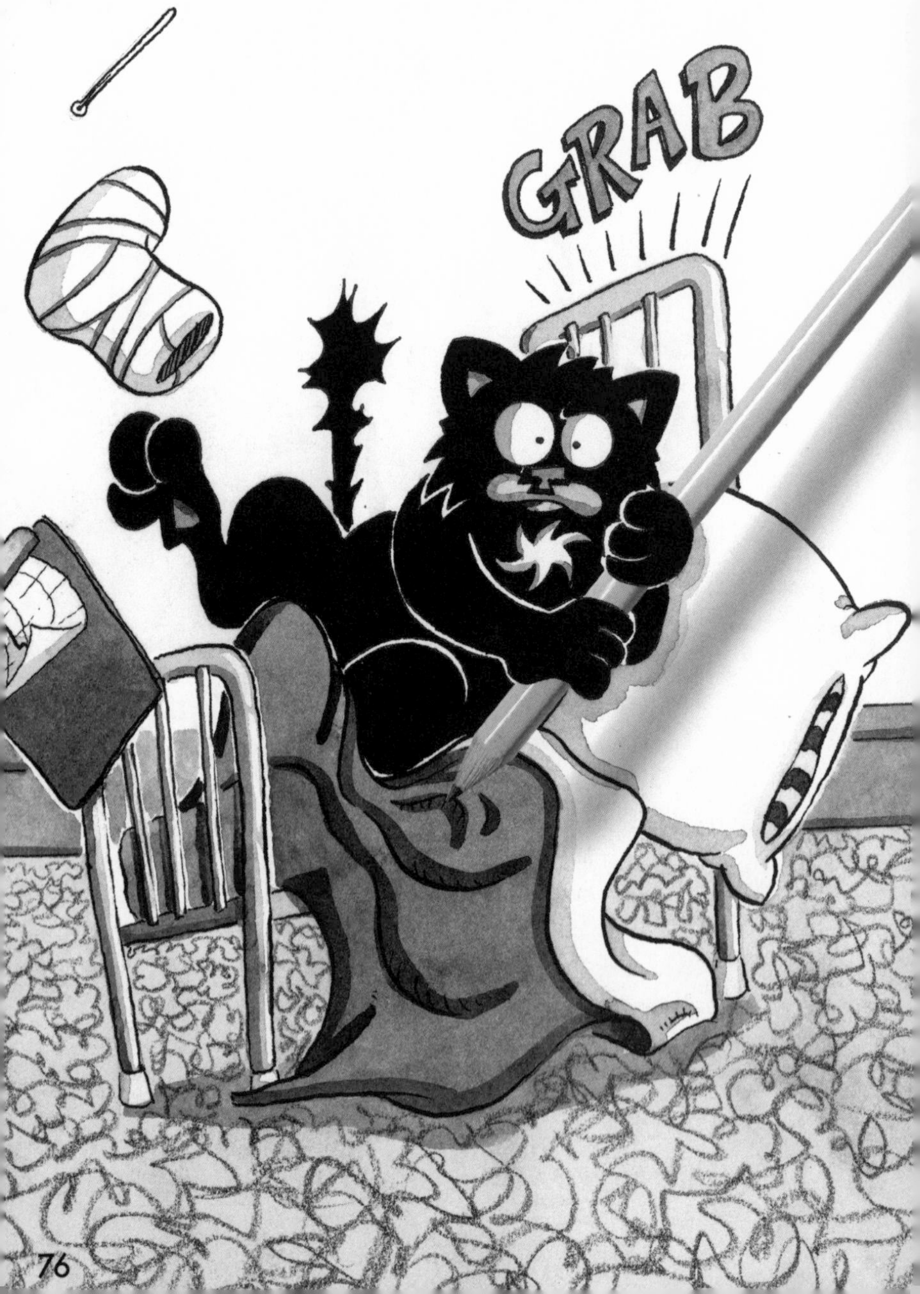
GRAB

KITTY! GIVE THAT BACK TO ME THIS INSTANT!

Oooooh! Sometimes you can be such a BAD KITTY!

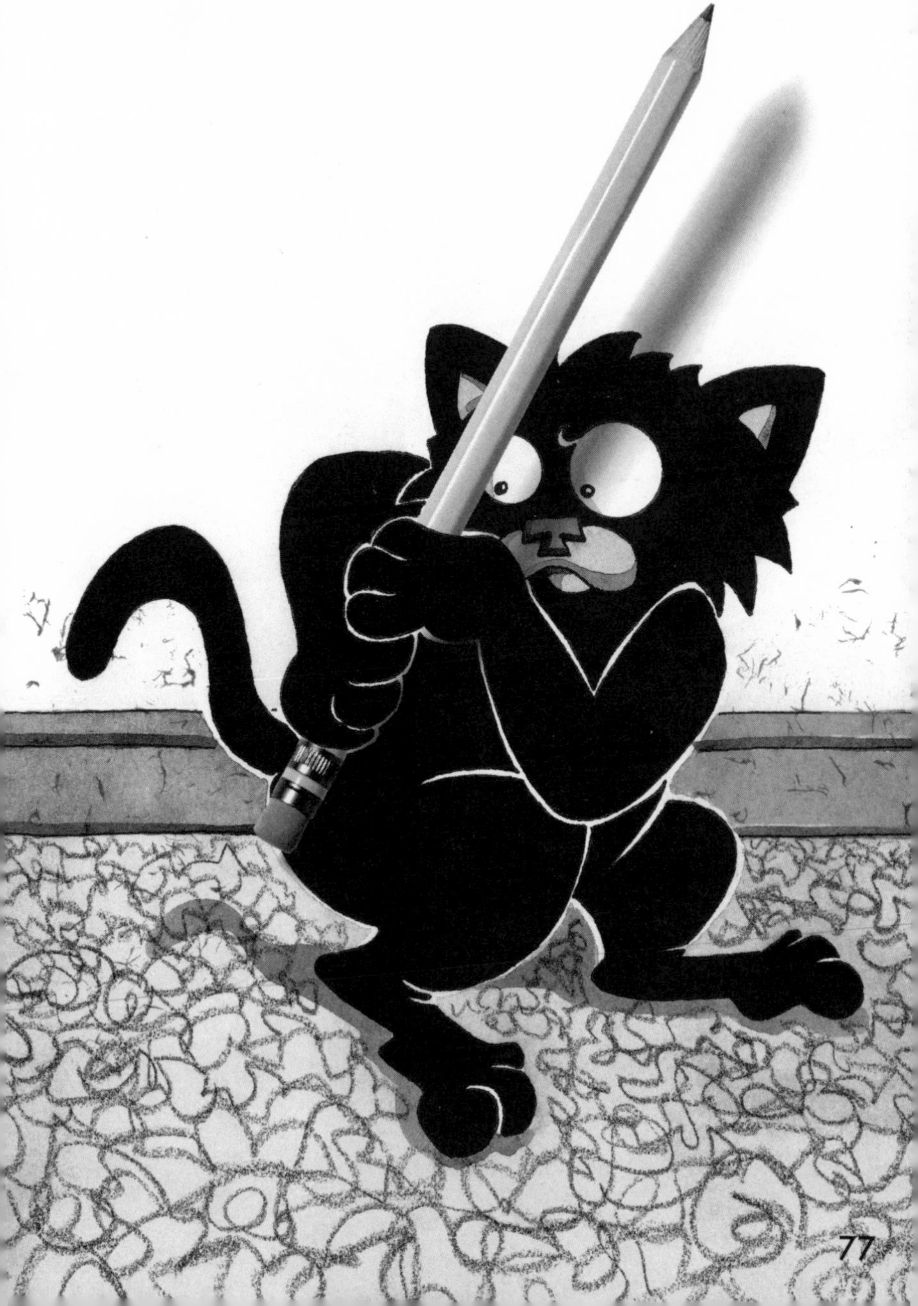

Oh, I see. You're still not happy with the plot of this story—YOUR story. Well, there's gratitude for you. Kitty, there's nothing that you can do about it now. Look, we're already on page 78!

Now what? You're packing?! Why? Where are you . . . Oh, I get it. You're running away. Well, that's mature.

Bon voyage, Kitty. You're doing me a favor, you know. You're giving the story another plot point. See, we started with a plot about you going on a diet. Then we added a plot point about you becoming sick from the shock of going on a diet.

And now you've added the plot point of you deciding to run away because you don't like your new
diet. Seems like a pretty good story to me so far.

Here, let me get the door for you.

But before you go, there's just one more thing . . .

LOOK OUT FOR THE GIANT OCTOPUS OUTSIDE THE DOOR!

The whole neighborhood has been overrun with them!

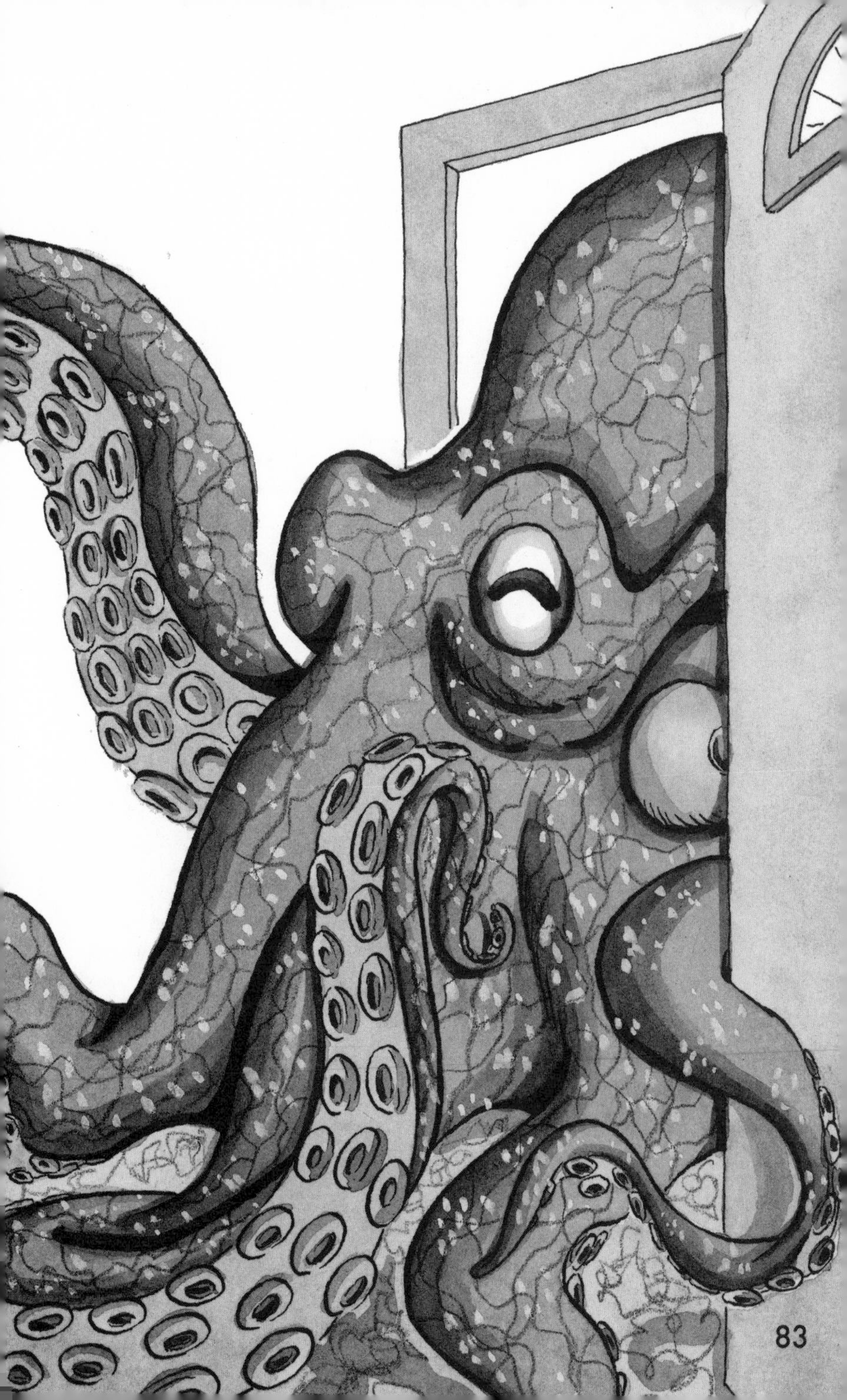

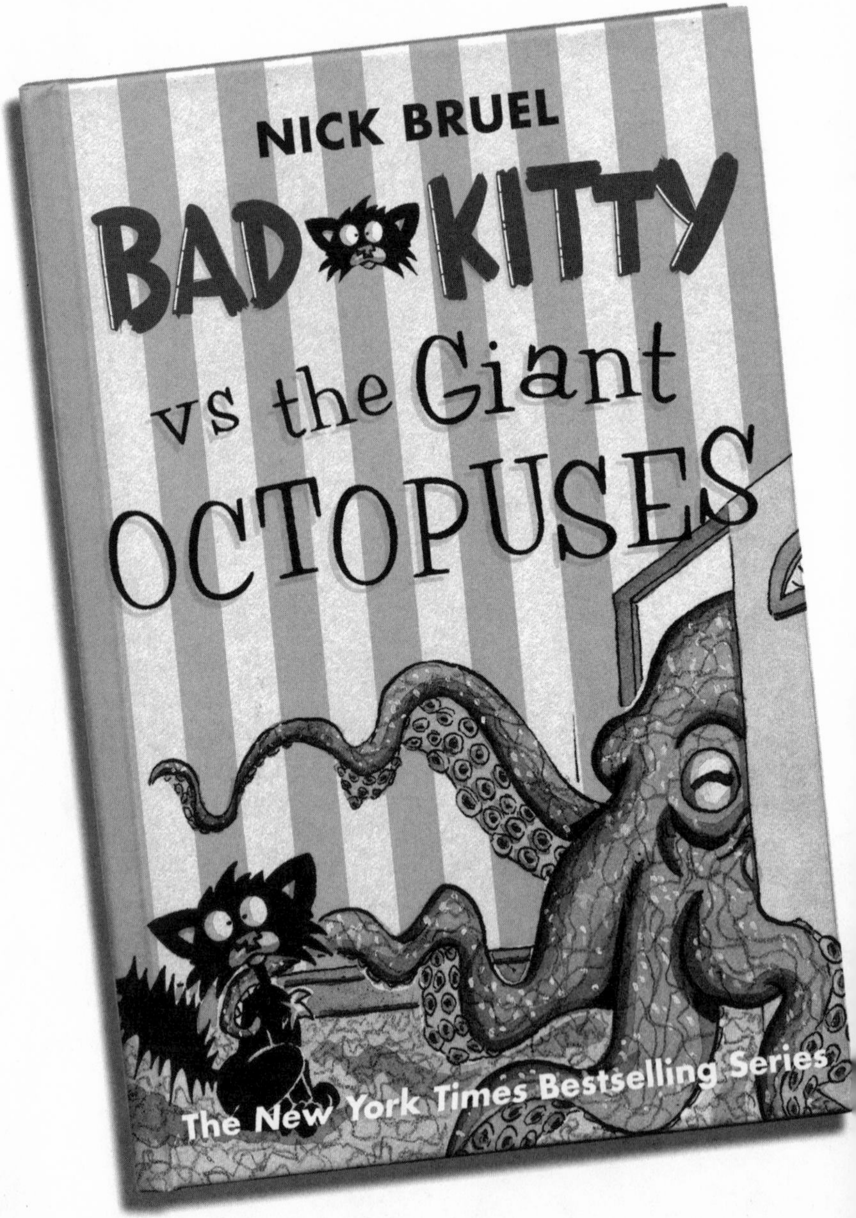
NICK BRUEL
BAD KITTY
vs the Giant
OCTOPUSES
The New York Times Bestselling Series

Wow! What a great title! I'd read a book with a title like that, wouldn't you, Kitty? It just goes to show that anything can happen in a story.

But there's just one thing bothering me . . . What is the plural of "octopus"? Is it "octopuses"? Or is it "octopi"?

Let's find out!

DON'T
ASK M

WHAT'S RIGHT "OCTOPUSES" OR "OCTOPI"?

So, Uncle Murray, which one is it?

Why are you asking me?

We always ask you stuff like this.

But this time, you can look it up for yourself!

dic·tion·ar·y - A book or electronic medium that contains a collection of words from any language listed in alphabetical order along with their spellings, meanings, pronunciations and other forms of use. In other words THIS is a dictionary

How?!

By using a DICTIONARY! Every writer NEEDS to have a dictionary for just this kind of question. Say you don't know how to spell a word. Look it up in a dictionary! Say you want to use a word in a story, but you're not sure if it's the right word. Look it up in a dictionary! A dictionary is a very important tool for any writer.

Cool! Are there any other important tools you can recommend?

Sure. Every writer should also have a THESAURUS. A thesaurus is a great book that helps you to find other words

that mean the same thing. When you look up a word in a thesaurus, you'll find lots of words that mean the same thing or something similar. And you can use these different words to help you make your story more interesting to read.

Say I write the sentence, "The boy walked to the store." By using a thesaurus and looking up some of the words, I can also write the same sentence as, "The lad perambulated to the boutique." But sometimes the fanciest words aren't the best words to use in your story. So, be careful.

Are there other kinds of dictionaries?

Sure! I sometimes use a RHYMING DICTIONARY when I'm writing poetry. When you look up a word in a rhyming dictionary, you find all of the other words that rhyme with it. For instance, there are lots and lots of words that rhyme with "Murray" like "hurry" and "blurry" and "scurry." But there are only a few words that rhyme with "Uncle." "Carbuncle" is one of them.

"Carbuncle"? What's that?!

Look it up in a dictionary! But don't do it on a full stomach. Trust me.

Oh, good. It looks like you've decided to stay, Kitty. I'm so pleased especially because we're getting so close to the end of our story.

Gosh, I would have been so sad . . . so very, very sad, if you had left this story before it ended.

Just . . . just thinking about it makes me . . .
sniff . . . get a little . . . sniffle . . . misty-eyed. SOB!
Oh, Kitty, I would have missed you SO MUCH!

Sorry about all
the tears, Kitty.

Which brings up a good point. All stories should include some emotion in them. A story can be funny or sad or . . .

... OR SCARY! DON'T FORGET SCARY!

Or scary. In fact, a good story should show more than one emotion in it because your readers have more than one emotion. People are not just happy or sad or angry or scared. They are all of those things and a lot more. So your characters should have lots of emotions, too.

By the way, a funny story can have sad parts if you want it to. And a sad story can even have funny bits if that's what you want. You can write your story however you want.

HEY, that reminds me of the most important rule about writing stories! I'll tell you all about it in the chapter I call . . .

YA LOUSY MUTT! I'VE BEEN LOOKING FOR THAT!

CHAPTER SIX

THE MOST IMPORTANT RULE ABOUT WRITING STORIES

Do you want to know what the most important rule about writing stories is, Kitty? Do you? Do you? Why aren't you answering me, Kitty?

Oh, that's right! You can't talk!

Well, I can fix that.

Thanks, Kitty! I'm so glad you're interested!

The most important rule to know about writing stories is easy.

It's YOUR story.

That's right, dear reader, when it's time for you to write YOUR story, that story will be YOURS and YOURS alone.

SURE! I'D LOVE TO KNOW!

This means that YOUR story can have as many characters or protagonists or antagonists as YOU want.

And you can have all of those characters do or say anything YOU want, because it's YOUR story.

And you can give your story any setting or as many settings as YOU want. By the way, this doesn't mean that your setting can be just in any PLACE that you want. You can set your story in any TIME that you want. Your story can be set in the past, the present, or even in the future.

Your story can have as much conflict and drama as you want. Your story can have as many plot points as you want.

The point is that you are the one in control of your story, just like I am here.

Kitty, I am so pleased that you're finally happy with your new diet!

TURNIPS MAKE ME HAPPY!

I think that your acceptance of your new diet may be the perfect ending to this story.

Really? Turnips?
I never thought I'd hear YOU say that!

Hi, Strange Kitty! You're here just in time! We were about to give this story an ending. As you know, every story needs an ending.

Oh! I see.

TURNIPS MAKE THE WORLD A BETTER PLACE!

I could have given this story any kind of ending. I could have ended this story with Kitty becoming so sick that she has to go to the hospital. But I didn't like that ending.

I'm a big turnip fan. For a second there, I thought you'd been reading my diary.

TURNIPS TASTE LIKE LOLLIPOPS!

MEOW! MEOW! MEOW!*

Really? Turnips?

*Turnips?! Did I hear someone mention turnips?

I could have ended this story with Kitty running away and never being seen again. Or I could have had her kidnapped by the octopus invaders and carried off to her doom. But I didn't like those endings either. Endings can be tricky.

Let's talk to Uncle Murray about endings. I'll bet he can tell us a few things!

Hi, Chatty. It wasn't Kitty. It was that Bruel guy.

I'LL NEVER GET TIRED OF TURNIPS!

MEOW MEOW* MEOW!

*Did you know that the first jack-o'-lanterns weren't made from pumpkins but from turnips? The Irish carved faces into turnips to ward off a spirit known as "Stingy Jack" who used a lump of burning coal placed inside of a hollowed-out turnip to light his way in the dark.

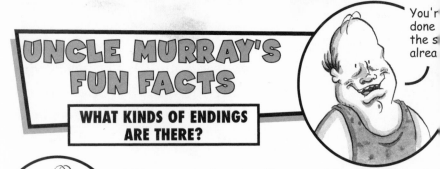

UNCLE MURRAY'S FUN FACTS

WHAT KINDS OF ENDINGS ARE THERE?

You'r
done
the s
alrea

There are basically two kinds of endings: CLOSED ENDINGS★ and OPEN ENDINGS.★

What's the difference?

Well, a closed ending is when you end a story in such a way that nothing more can happen. An open ending is when you end a story, but you leave a little something there that makes a reader wonder if maybe more could happen.

But that makes an open ending sound like it's not an ending at all.

Okay, I'll give you an example. Say you have a story about a handsome super-hero—let's call him Super Murray—and he has the power to fly, travel through time, turn invisible, and shoot powerful laser beams out of his eyes. At the end of the story, Super Murray beats up the villain and saves the city. The villain goes to jail, a really pretty lady falls in love with

106

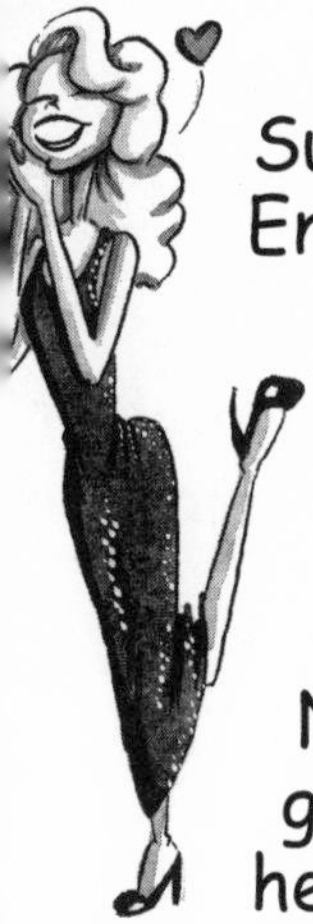

Super Murray, and everybody is safe. The End. That would be a CLOSED ending, because there's no more story to tell.

Something tells me you've been thinking about this a lot.

Now let's say that instead of the villain going to jail, he escapes and the last thing he says is, "You've won this battle, Super Murray, but tomorrow is another day!" And then he limps away with a menacing chuckle that sounds like "Heh-heh-heh!" In this version, the story still ends with Super Murray saving the city, the pretty lady falling in love with him, and the villain being defeated, but now the reader is left to wonder about what the villain might do next. That is an OPEN ending.

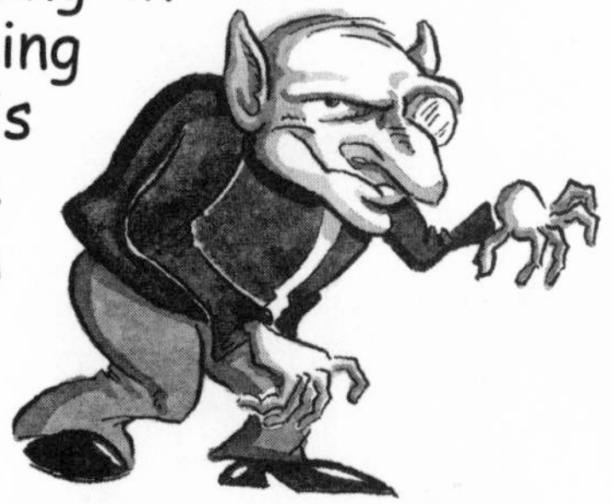

You've REALLY been thinking about this a lot.

Open endings are a great way to create a series in which one story leads to the next. And then the whole series can have its own title. Something like . . . "The Astounding Adventures of Super Murray." Or . . . you know . . . whatever.

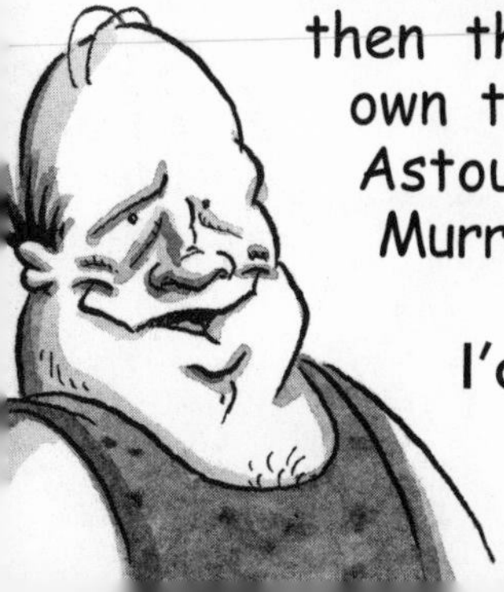

I'd read it. Thanks, Super Murray . . . I mean, Uncle Murray.

Oh, great! The whole gang is here. You're all just in time for the ending of this story.

Kitty needed to lose some weight, so she went on a turnip diet. She didn't like it and got sick because of it.

She even ran away. But the octopus invasion convinced her to stay.

And now she loves turnips more than anything!

THE END

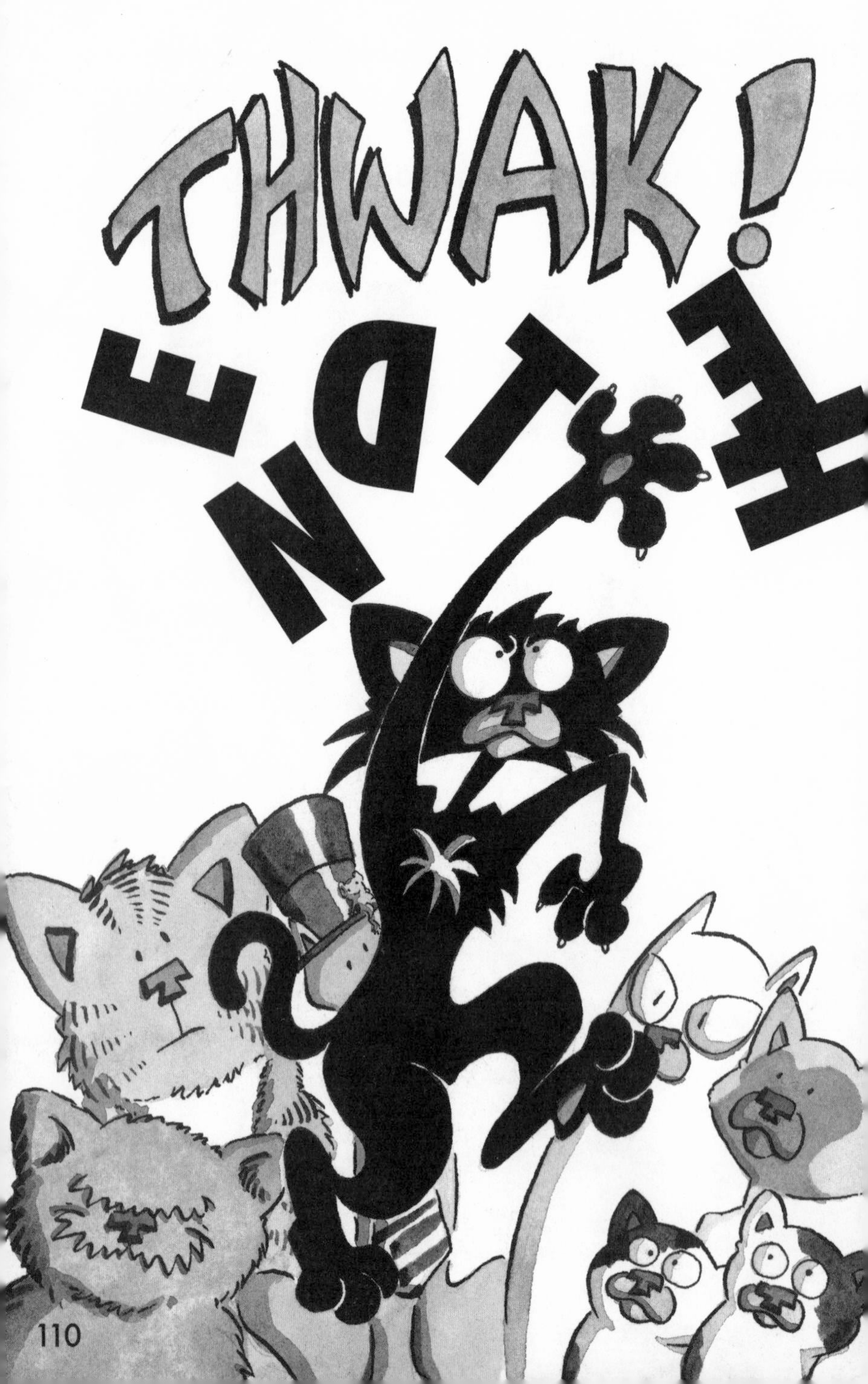
THWAK!

OH, COME ON, KITTY! The story is over! There's nothing you can do about it! Absolutely nothing! From now on, you're a cat who loves turnips. Just accept it!

Maybe in your next book, you can convince all of the other kitties to eat turnips, too! Wouldn't that be fun? Wouldn't it?

Uh . . . What's going on?

Kitty . . . Why are you looking at me like that?

What are you thinking?

Kitty? Kitty?

Back up, cats.
Slowly . . .
Slowly . . .

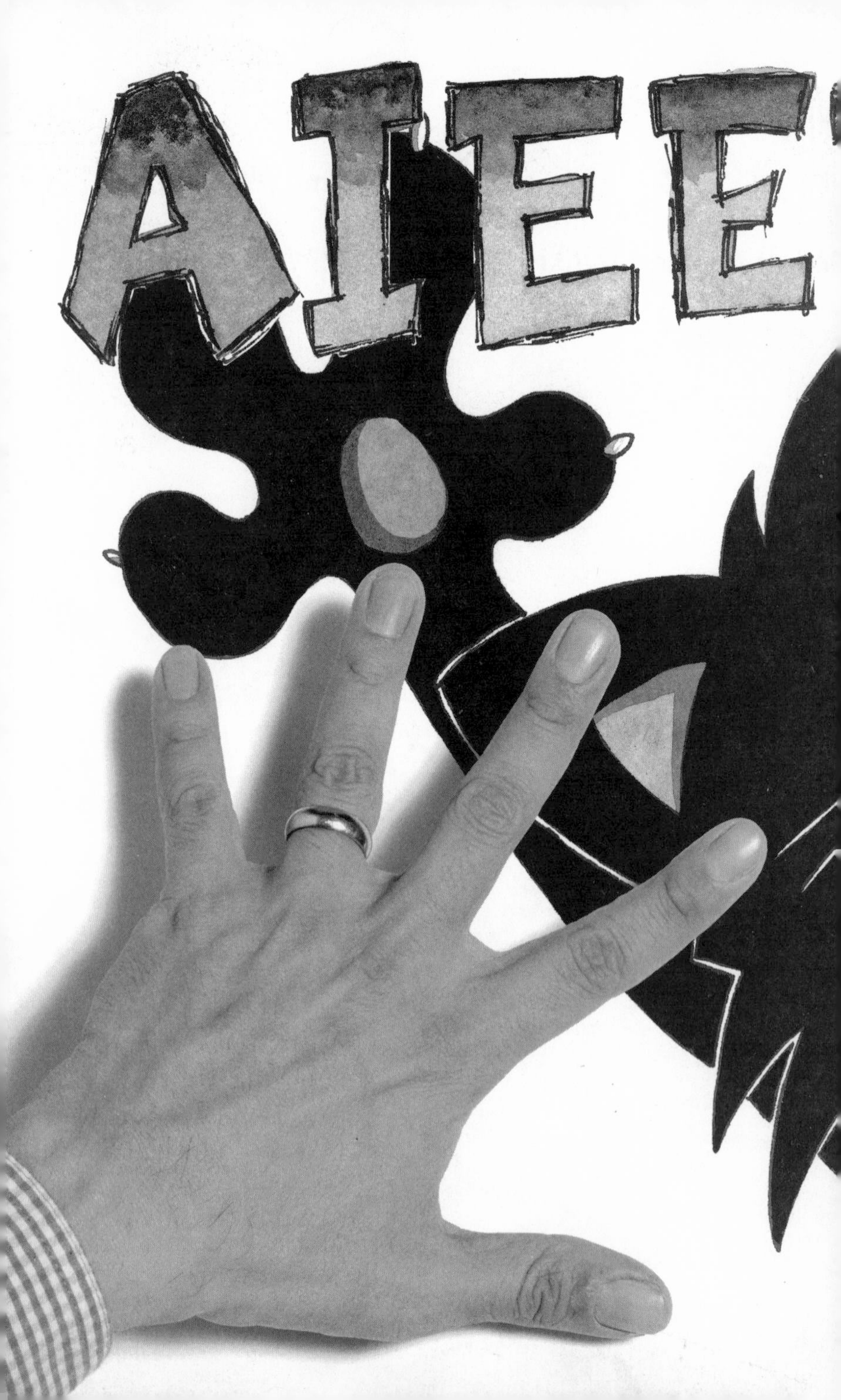
AIEE

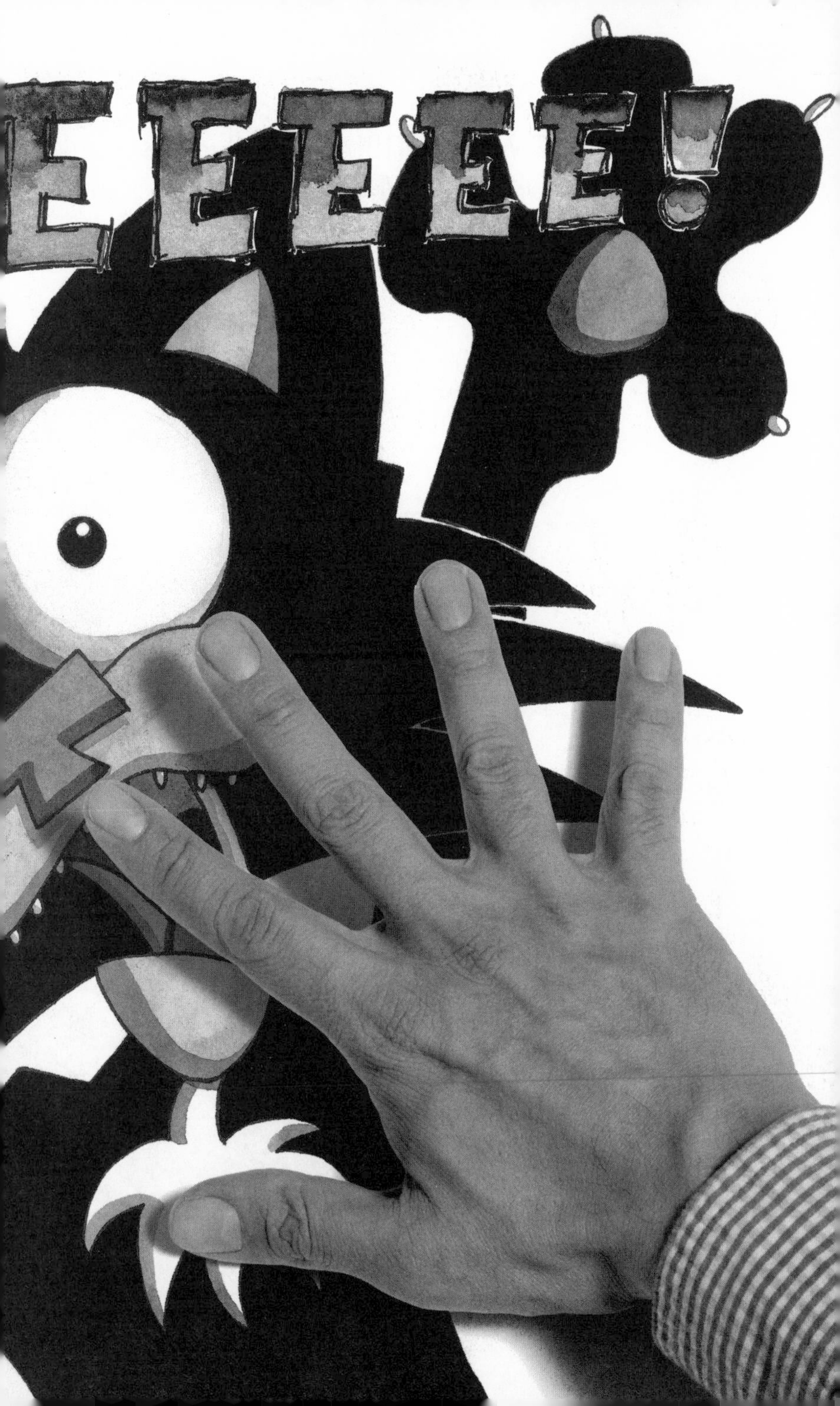
EEEEE!

I've . . . OUCH! . . . I've given it some thought, Kitty
And I've . . . OW, MY TIBIA! . . . I've decided that
there's . . . CHOKE . . . Why is it so dark in here . . . ?
I've decided that there's another option.

• EPILOGUE★ •

COUGH . . . OUCH . . . Well, Kitty. You did such a nice job . . . Gosh, it's dark in here . . . such a nice job with your diet, that you deserve . . . So cold, so very, very cold . . . you deserve a treat.

Bon appétit, Kitty.

I'll be seeking some medical attention now.

And now, the Appendix.

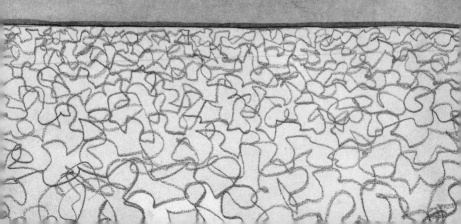

· APPENDIX ·

A glossary of important terms covered in this book, placed in the order in which they appear.

Author An incredibly beautiful person who writes books and always smells like lavender, even in hot weather.

Illustrator An incredibly beautiful and fragrant person who creates the artwork for a book. Often, the author and the illustrator of a book are the same person.

Character An individual inside a story who expresses thoughts or is committed to action. In this story, every individual we meet is a character including Kitty, Puppy, the zombie, and the brilliant octopus, because characters do not necessarily have to have names to appear in a story.

Protagonist The main character in a story. The protagonist in this story was Kitty, since we followed her actions more than any other character.

Foreshadowing A device in which an author can drop little hints that will alert readers to events that may happen later in the story. The example of the zombie dropping on the floor hinted at the unfortunate collapse.

Setting The place or time in which a story occurs. A story may have many settings. The setting for this story was mostly Kitty's home.

MacGuffin This is a term coined for films, but suitable for any type of story to describe an important goal of the protagonist. It can take the form of an object and result from the protagonist trying to obtain a certain item that the protagonist hopes to gain. The MacGuffin was her breakfast, and it was her desire to get her food that gave the reader a better understanding of Kitty herself.

HOLD IT!

STOP THE APPENDIX

STOP! BASTA! ¡ALTO! ARRETEZ!

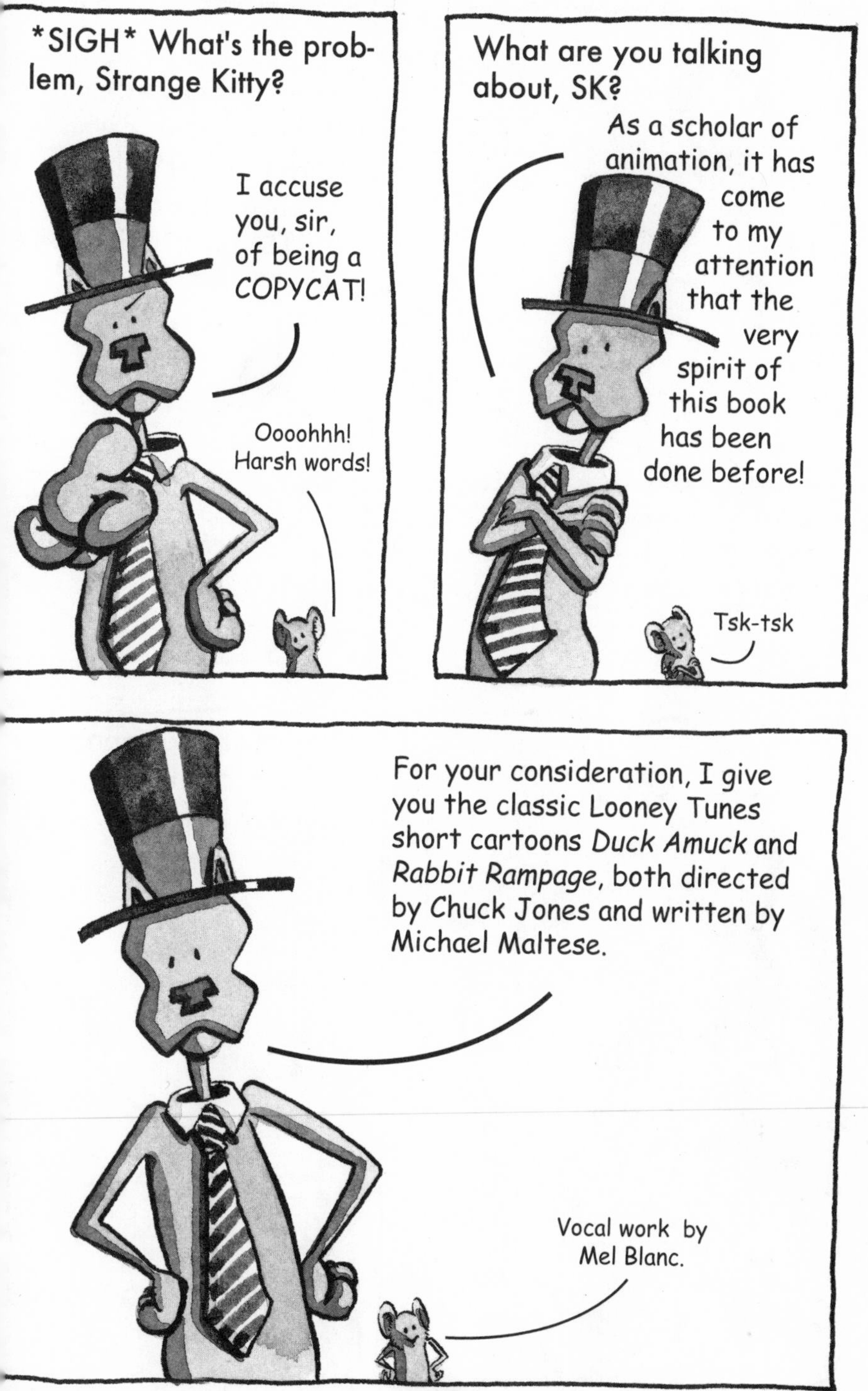
SIGH What's the problem, Strange Kitty?
I accuse you, sir, of being a COPYCAT!
Oooohhh! Harsh words!
What are you talking about, SK?
As a scholar of animation, it has come to my attention that the very spirit of this book has been done before!
Tsk-tsk
For your consideration, I give you the classic Looney Tunes short cartoons *Duck Amuck* and *Rabbit Rampage*, both directed by Chuck Jones and written by Michael Maltese.
Vocal work by Mel Blanc.

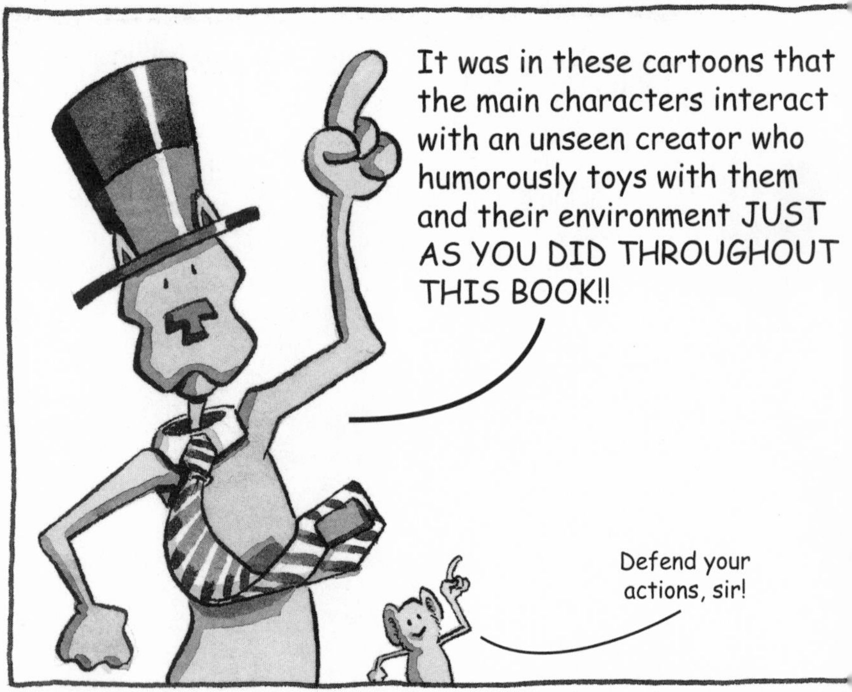
It was in these cartoons that the main characters interact with an unseen creator who humorously toys with them and their environment JUST AS YOU DID THROUGHOUT THIS BOOK!!
Defend your actions, sir!

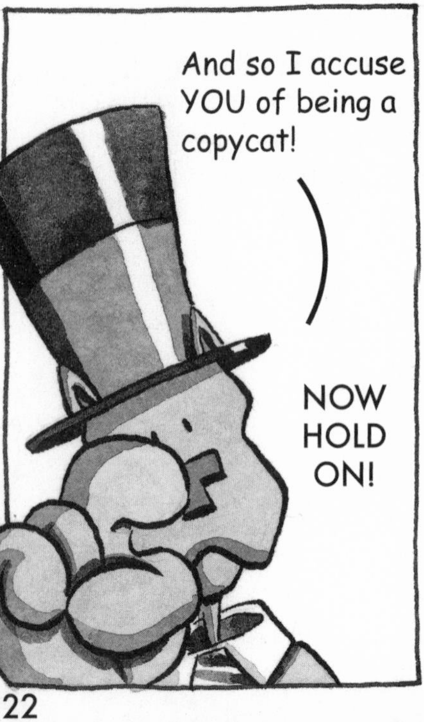
And so I accuse YOU of being a copycat!
NOW HOLD ON!

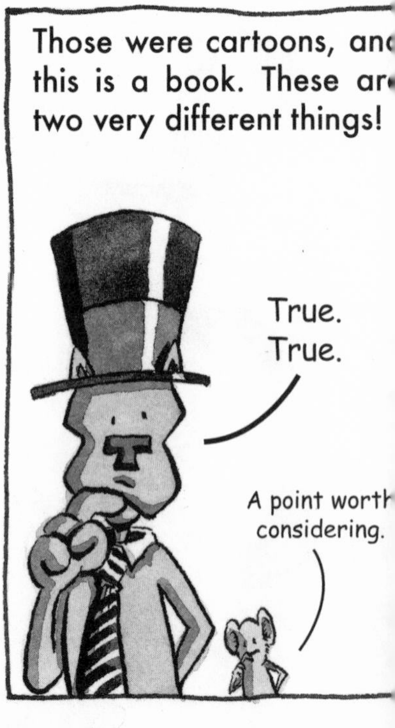
Those were cartoons, an
this is a book. These ar
two very different things!
True. True.
A point wort
considering.

But I agree with you.

AHA!

J'accuse!

I was inspired by those cartoons to make this book. But I didn't copy them. Copying is wrong.

Go on.
Go on.

Yes, go on.

All art is inspired by the art that comes before it. Even *Duck Amuck* has similarities to *Gertie the Dinosaur* by Winsor McKay, which was created thirty-nine years earlier.

Hadn't thought of that.

Oops.

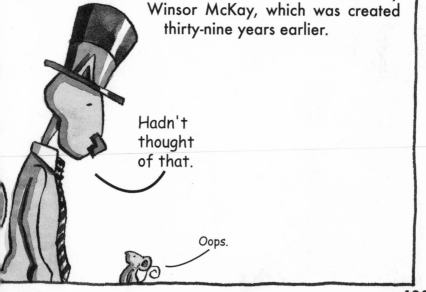

In fact, nothing would make me happier than to know that someone will read this book and become inspired to make their own Bad Kitty books.

Who's that?!

Nick —
Please don't tell readers to make their own Bad Kitty stories. We want them to read OUR Bad Kitty books.
Neal

Nice penmanship.

That's my editor. Sorry, Neal, but I don't want to be the only one having fun making Bad Kitty books.

Hey, LOOK! There's a kid over there getting out a pen and some paper!

There's another one! And another!